# A MONSTER

To Eric and Monty with love
~ T. K.

For Violet Léone xx
~ L. S.

**tiger tales**
5 River Road, Suite 128, Wilton, CT 06897
Published in the United States 2015
Originally published in Great Britain 2015
by Little Tiger Press
Text copyright © 2015 Timothy Knapman
Illustrations copyright © 2015 Loretta Schauer
ISBN-13: 978-1-58925-176-2
ISBN-10: 1-58925-176-8
Printed in China
LTP/1400/0987/0914

For more insight and activities,
visit us at www.tigertalesbooks.com

# MOVED IN!

BY

TIMOTHY KNAPMAN

ILLUSTRATED BY

LORETTA SCHAUER

tiger tales

It was summer, but it was raining.
So **Ben** was stuck inside
with **NOTHING** to do.

"Read a book,"
said Dad.

"Build a rocket,"
said Mom.

"Go and look for dragons in the spare bedroom," said **Dad**.
"There's no such thing as dragons!" said Ben.
But then he had a **WONDERFUL** idea.

"I'm going to make a fort,"
he said.

"But a monster might move in!"
said **Mom** and **Dad** together.

"Don't be silly!"
said Ben.

He made an AMAZING fort.
It wasn't an outside fort made of sticks and dirt and leaves.
You'd expect a **monster** to move in *there*.
It was an inside fort, made of cushions
and pillows, with a rug on top.
Far too cozy for

**monsters.**

Still, **Ben** got
his ray blaster and his
shining armor shield,
**JUST IN CASE.**

But nothing the least bit exciting happened.
It just rained and rained.

Ben tried being a
**PIRATE** on the lookout
for ships to plunder . . .

A sword-fighting **KNIGHT**
in his great castle . . . .

A **WIZARD** in his cave
of wonders . . . .

But it wasn't much fun on his own.
*Sometimes, I wish a monster WOULD move in!* thought Ben.

BIG MISTAKE!

"I don't believe it!"
said Ben . . . .

"A **monster** moved in!"

"Told you so!"
said Mom and Dad.

"Hmph!"
said Ben.

The **monster** didn't look very scary.
His T-shirt said that his name was Burple.
So **Ben** was brave and joined him in the fort.
*He seems harmless,*
thought **Ben**.

Suddenly, **Burple** started

HOWLING

so LOUDLY

that

Ben's ears

hurt.

Then

Burple's

DISGU

# STING

**PACKED LUNCH** escaped and tried to eat the fort.

So they both had to sit on it until it stopped moving.

"This is no fun at all!" said **Ben**.

"I'm sorry, but it's summer and it's raining so there's nothing to do," said **Burple**.

That reminded **Ben** of something, and he had a **GREAT** idea.

He read a book to **Burple**, and **Burple** said, "WOW! Let's read another!"

Then he and **Burple** built a rocket, and **Burple** said,

"COOL! Let's blast off!"

And then they went to look for **DRAGONS** in the spare room.

BIG
MISTAKE!

But when the smoke cleared,
**Burple** said,
"Yay! That was fun!"

The rain had stopped, so they took **Burple's DISGUSTING PACKED LUNCH** for a walk in the park.

It chased sticks while they hung
upside down and told each other jokes.
Ben and Burple laughed so much
that their sides hurt.

Ben wished Burple could
stay forever.

But soon it was time
for him to go home.

"This was my best day ever!"
said **Burple**.

"Mine too," said Ben.
"Thank you for coming."

The next day, it was sunny but there was **NOTHING** to do.

And then **Burple** had a **WONDERFUL** idea.

"I'm going to make a fort,"
he said.

"But a **boy** might move in!"
said his **Mom** and **Dad** together.

"I hope so!"
said **Burple**.

And he did!